D0589886

Please return/renew this item by the
last date shown to avoid a charge.
Books may also be renewed by phone
and Internet. May not be renewed if
required by another reader.

www.libraries.barnet.gov.uk

nchley Crouch End

020 8359 3800

THE WHALE WATCHERS

DOUGIE POYNTER

Illustrated by AMBERIN HUQ

A message from the author

I'm really pleased you have picked up this book because that means you might share my love of nature and that you're up for learning more.

I'm so excited to share The Whale Watchers with you, a book that shows us all how whales are so important in the fight against climate change, why protecting them and their environment is so key and what YOU can do to make a difference too! It has been a real adventure for me, discovering the impact whales have on the world around them, and I can't wait to share THIS awesome adventure with you.

Unfortunately, humans are now producing more plastic waste than ever and, despite many people working hard to reduce the impact they make, there are actually loads of animals out there helping to make a difference through their everyday lives - we just don't know it!

Few animals do more for our climate than whales and it has been really cool to work with amazing scientists to learn all about them.

I've always loved animals and really care about the impact we have on their habitats and the natural world. I've been lucky enough to bring this passion into my music and in my writing as an author. I'm totally committed to cleaning up our planet and doing whatever I can to help the environment.

I hope the different ways we explore cutting down single-use plastic in this book inspires you to do the same and help protect our environment.

Now is the time to act; if we all make small changes, together we can make a big difference.

Peace out,

The Whale Watchers

Chapter 1

Sleeper Train To Nowhere

As Finn dragged his wheelie bag along the platform towards the 9.15 p.m. sleeper train from London Euston to Inverness, he wondered if this could be the **worst summer holiday** that anyone in the **whole history of summer holidays** had ever been forced to go on. His mum shouted and waved at him from a doorway a few carriages ahead. **"It's this one!"** she said. His little brother Jesse's head popped out next to her, his face scrunched into a frown. **"Come ON, Finny!"** he shouted, before they both disappeared into the train.

Finn sighed. They'd had bad summer holidays before, of course. There'd been that one in Spain not long after their dad had left, where the pool had turned a funny greenish colour and all the kids got sick, and Finn and his brother spent most of the holiday in their room throwing up while Mum pretended not to cry.

They'd been on other work holidays with Mum before too, a few field trips to Cornwall, and one to study the dolphins in Cardigan Bay in Wales.

But at least in those places there'd been a **teeny tiny** chance of sunshine, and maybe even jumping in the sea without getting **hypothermia**. Neither of them was exactly Spain, but they weren't up by the North Pole either.

This time, Mum had really done it, thought Finn as he heaved his bag up on to the train that would be taking them north, all through the night, through the whole of England and most of Scotland, about as far north as it was possible to go without hitting the sea on the other side. Temperature-wise, they might as well be going to **Siberia**. And they weren't even going to the *sea* – just an estuary, or an "inlet", as his mum had called it: the Moray Firth, a great big split in the north-east of Scotland where the sea snaked in.

Finn couldn't be less excited if he tried. He yawned and followed the sound of his brother's voice down the train carriage, between the pairs of seats on one side and the single seats on the other. Jesse stood in the aisle, clutching his **Little**

5

Book of Big Whales, and talking very seriously to a man in a suit sitting across from Mum.

"Hello, I'm Jesse. We're going to **Scopland** to see whales and I'm going to see a humpback whale, NOT just minke whales like Mum, because humpbacks are **my favourite**, even though they're not as big as blue whales, but I still like them the best because—"

"It's *Scot*land, love," said Mum, "now come and sit down ..."

The man in the suit was smiling, but Finn thought he looked a little tense. It was going to be a long journey, after all, and not everyone liked whales as much as Jesse did.

Of course, they could have *flown* to Inverness in an hour and a half, but his

mum would never have allowed that, not when it was such a short distance and there was a perfectly good train they could catch with a much lighter carbon footprint. Finn had at least hoped that Mum might get them all a bed – a bed on a train might *almost* have been fun – but no. By the looks of it, a seat on an all-night train it was.

"I thought you'd appreciate the single seat," said Mum with a wink, indicating the one across the aisle from hers and Jesse's.

Finn nodded and shoved his bag on the rack above his head. The man in the suit was sitting behind him. The cracks in his smile were beginning to show as Jesse continued to offload everything he knew about humpback whales. Finn couldn't help but smile. When it came to whales, Jesse could talk for England, and Scotland too.

"And did you know humpbacks aren't the biggest whales but they DO have the biggest pectoral fins, which are the ones on the side, and HUGE tails which means they can swim **really, really fast** and **really, really far**, and they live ALL OVER the world, in ALL the oceans," Jesse was explaining, "so you CAN see them in Scopland, or in Greenland, or in Hawaii even, or in the Arctic, or—"

"Excuse me," said Mum, leaning across the aisle,

"if anybody here likes peanut butter sandwiches, they'd better get to their seat right away, especially if they want the window seat."

Jesse immediately leapt into the window seat and waited with his hands out for Mum to pass him his sandwich. She handed one to Finn too, from her Tupperware tubs, as usual, along with a refillable water bottle and an apple.

Finn rolled his eyes. The man behind him had a big plastic bag from the station shop, filled with drinks and snacks no doubt. Finn could hear the rustling of crisp packets and the fizz of his drink when he unscrewed the top.

"I don't know why we can't just buy a drink and a sandwich in the station like everyone else," Finn muttered.

"Yes, you do," said his mum in a quiet voice.

"Because the plastic goes into the ocean and it hurts whales," recited Jesse with a mouth full of peanut butter, "*and* fish and seabirds and other animals like turtles and seals and ..."

Finn nodded but he wasn't really listening. He'd heard this one **a million times**. It's not that he didn't believe it. He did. He knew it was true. He knew about the whales all around the world that were washing up on beaches, their **stomachs filled with plastic**, the crabs found trapped inside scrunched-up plastic cups, the seabirds choking on plastic bags and plastic bottle tops. He'd seen all the pictures, scrolled horrified through the news stories on his phone. He knew all the tragedies of his mum's work as a marine biologist.

Even in London – even fifty miles from the nearest sea – they weren't safe from it.

They had all been there to witness the terrible death of the little minke whale in the River Thames last year. Finn and Jesse had watched from the bridge with the rest of the onlookers, everyone laughing and excited at first to witness this beautiful sea creature's big day out in the city. But then the mood had changed as it slowly dawned on the crowd that the whale was sick, that it wasn't meant to be there, that it wasn't going to make it back to the sea. Mum had been called down to help. But even with all her knowledge, there was nothing she could do – *there's never anything anyone can do*, thought Finn – and in the end, the whale had to be put down, and Jesse had cried and cried and the knot in Finn's stomach had got that bit tighter.

Why did Mum put them all through it when it was clearly **hopeless?**

What was the point in avoiding plastic bags and plastic packaging and plastic bottles? What difference did not buying a drink and a sandwich at the station *really* make? Plastic was already everywhere. Didn't she see? It was *too late*.

And what was the point in dragging them to the **end of nowhere** to study these beautiful, majestic creatures of the deep when it was so obvious that we were slowly wiping them out, like we were wiping out ALL the animals, like we were wiping out ourselves too, and our entire planet, and—

Finn felt a hand on his knee. His mum was smiling across at him.

"You OK, love?"

"I'm fine," said Finn. He looked down at his hands which he realised were fists.

Mum squeezed his knee. "Get some sleep, love," she said, settling back into her own seat.

Finn stretched out his fingers and took a few deep breaths, like he'd been told to do, and tried his best to relax.

How the little whale had ended up in the Thames, no one really knew. Had her mum died some terrible untimely death, leaving her to fend for herself? Did she get lost? Was she sick? Was she scared by something, or was she hungry, her food supplies low, her waters polluted?

Whatever the reason, to Finn it had felt like she had been purposefully seeking them out, like she had some dark message to deliver – a cry for help, or a warning of impending doom.

Finn took his glasses off and rubbed at his face, like he was trying to rub out the thought, erase the images of **dying animals** and **plastic-polluted *seas*** that had haunted him since. He suddenly felt very tired. He rested his head against the window and as the train rumbled out of Euston station and into the twilit evening beyond – the glow of office-block windows and streetlamps and traffic lights shining out from the darkening sky – he noticed, without surprise, that it was raining.

Great, he thought.

He wished more than anything that he was on a plane, flying *south*, flying miles away from bad weather and bad news, rather than travelling deeper into it. He wished they were off to some sunny resort with a bright blue swimming pool and a diving board and rows of sunbeds and a bar that served French fries and brightly coloured fizzy drinks with umbrellas in them, the sort of place where you might forget about the real world for a while.

But the gentle tapping of the rain against the window and the steady **da-dum da-dum** of the train as it chugged along the tracks was strangely soothing, and it wasn't long before his eyes grew heavy and he slipped into a deep, dark sleep.

Chapter 2

Watch Where You're Going

Finn squinted against the morning light as they stepped off the train. Mum's colleague Jim was waving at them from the other end of the platform. He was a large and friendly man, who gave them all enthusiastic hugs and backslaps and led them to his car where Finn and Jesse climbed into the back and promptly fell asleep again to the sound of Mum and Jim chatting quietly in the front.

The next thing Finn knew, he was waking to the bump and scrunch of tyres turning into a gravel driveway and Mum's voice saying, "OK, kids, we're here."

Jim turned the engine off, and swivelled round, beaming. "Not a bad spot, eh?"

Finn yawned and stretched and stepped out of the car. Immediately a cool wind **swirled** around him, lifting the hair off his neck.

He had to admit, it *wasn't* bad. The cottage itself was tiny – all white walls and wooden beams – but it was *right* on the beach. Grass-covered sand dunes rose up behind and around it, sheltering it from the wind, and in front, the sand sloped away towards the water. The sun had even come out, though with the wind, it wasn't exactly *warm*. The wind brought other things, though – a liveliness, the sound of gulls arcing overhead, and a smell ...

Salt, Finn realised. "I thought this *wasn't* the sea?" he asked.

"Aye, it is," said Jim, getting their bags out of the boot, "and the more so the further out you go. We're still at the Inner Moray here. Out there" – he pointed off to the right – "that's the Outer Moray, where it meets the North Sea. That's where your mum'll be on the boat no doubt."

Jesse was already stomping off down the path towards the beach. He was making noises to himself and he had thrown his arms out to the side, like a plane.

"Not too far, Jesse!" Mum called after him.

Jim smiled. "Need help bringing the bags in?"

"No, we're fine, thanks, Jim," said Mum. "Sure you don't mind looking in on the boys tomorrow?"

"Course not! We'll have some fun, won't we?" He gave Finn a wink and got back in the car. "And don't forget the **beach clean** next week! We always get a good turnout for that, especially if the weather's fine."

Finn tried his best to smile as they waved Jim off, but inside he felt his spirits sinking. Was a beach clean really their idea of fun round here?

Mum put a hand on Finn's shoulder.

"We'll be OK here, won't we, love?" she asked, squinting across at him. "I know it's not France, but—"

"It's fine, Mum," said Finn, shrugging off her hand. Then feeling bad, he added, "It's great." He carried his bag up to the front door.

24

Mum watched him go. "You sure you're OK, love? I know—"

"Mum, I'm fine, honestly," he said. "Just a bit tired."

After a moment, Mum nodded. "Grab your brother, would you?" she said. "I'll open up and put the kettle on."

Finn walked down the gravel path towards the sparkling water below. As he moved out of the protection of the dunes, the wind tore across him. It **slapped** his cheeks and threw his hair across his face, as if it was trying to wake him up.

The beach was much bigger than Finn had imagined. Miles of sand stretched away in both directions, and the sea in front of him was lively and choppy, a mass of little waves whipped up by the wind. Looking across the water, you could see

the other bank of the Moray Firth, but to
the right – to the east, where the morning
sun was hanging low above the water –
the two banks grew steadily further apart
as they widened into the Outer Moray, and
the sea. The sun threw down **a golden
path** across the water to where Finn was
standing, like an invitation.

Finn was walking towards it in a trance
when someone **crashed** straight into
him, knocking his glasses clean off
his face.

"Watch where you're going, would you?" said a voice.

Finn groped for his glasses in the sand, blinded for a moment. He put them back on then turned angrily towards his assailant.

It was a girl, probably about the same age as him. She had wild, **wind-blown hair** and a **furious** scowl on her face that could have turned a kitten to stone. Finn only caught a glimpse of this scowl, as the girl didn't bother to stop. She just threw it over her shoulder, like an insult, then carried on storming down the beach.

A brown shaggy dog was trotting after her and around her neck, Finn noticed, was a pair of binoculars.

"You ran into ME!" he shouted after her, but she was already gone.

Chapter 3

An Arrow-shaped Scar

When they got back to the cottage and Finn learnt that he would be sharing a room with his brother for the next six weeks, he mentally added it to the **growing** list of things that were wrong with this holiday.

Their room was tiny, like the rest of the house – little more than twin beds each pushed up against a wall – but one of the beds had a window next to it. Finn sat on the bed and looked out. The window looked east, towards the sea.

Jesse eyed him from the doorway. "Why do you get that bed?"

"Because I'm the oldest."

"OK, *fine*," said Jesse after a moment, "but only if you **promise** we can look for whales tomorrow."

Finn pretended to think very hard about this, then agreed. It's not like he wouldn't be forced to do it anyway.

After they'd had some lunch and unpacked their bags, Jesse lay on his bed and soon fell asleep still reading his *Little Book of Big Whales*, thumb in mouth. Finn took the moment of quiet to lie down too. He undid the latch on the window next to his bed and pushed it open.

From his lying down position, Finn couldn't see the sea, but he could smell it, and on his back with his eyes closed, he could hear the **swish** of the wind in the grasses and the **crash** of the waves

on the sand and the **twittering** and
squawking and **cawing** of a million
different birds. The world outside sounded
so lively and awake that Finn wondered
if he'd be able to get to sleep, and for a
minute he thought maybe he'd just get up
and go for a walk, but then he must have
drifted off because when he opened his
eyes again the sky through the window
was grey, and it was raining.

Jesse was still fast asleep, so Finn
slipped out of bed and closed the door
quietly behind him. In the front room, his
mum was hunched over the big dining
room table. Her paperwork was spread
out over it – a series of photos of whales
and close-ups of dorsal fins.

"Oh hello, love," she said, glancing
back at him. "Can I get you something?

There's some biscuits in the kitchen, and bread if you want toast."

"I'll get it," he said.

"Thanks, love."

He peered over her shoulder at the photos. "They all look the same," he said.

"Ahh, but they're not!" she said. "Look at the markings on this minke whale's fin – they're quite distinctive … like parallel lines, see? Now look at this one." She showed him the two photos.

"So your job is to try and spot these whales?"

"Exactly. By identifying particular whales and tracking their position and movement through UK waters, we can build up a picture of their behaviours and habits – where they go, what they eat, where they breed. It's particularly

important for minke whales, as we know
so little about them, much less than about
humpback whales, for instance."

Finn picked up one of the photos.
"This scar looks like an **arrow**," he said,
looking at the triangular-shaped mark on
the whale's dorsal fin.

"Well spotted!" said Mum, smiling up

at him. "That's what they've named him – Arrow. He's a juvenile. He and his mum have been sighted regularly in these waters over the past few years, but neither of them have been seen for a while."

"Probably dead then," Finn muttered.

Mum scraped her chair back and turned to face him, a look of concern on her face. Finn headed for the kitchen, hoping to brush the moment away, but she caught his hand.

"Come and sit with me a minute," she said. She pulled out the chair next to her and patted it.

Finn sighed and sat down. He knew what was coming, he felt the tugging, tightening inside.

Mum took a deep breath, as if working out where to start. "I know that little minke in the Thames really upset you," she said, putting her hand on his. "I know it's hard on you, what I do."

"It's fine, Mum," he said, pulling his hand away. "I just wish we could go on a *normal* holiday and just ... forget about this stuff for a while."

"I know you do," Mum said, staring into her lap. "Sometimes I wish I could too. I know these things are not easy to face – the climate crisis, plastic pollution, our effect on our environment. I know it's upsetting."

"It's not, I mean, it *is*, but it's just ... **pointless**."

Mum looked at him. "Why is it pointless?"

"Because nothing's going to change. People **won't** stop using plastic. The sea is full of it already and the whales are all *dying*, like the elephants and the tigers and the turtles and all the other animals we've killed."

"Whales are not all dying, Finn! Yes, some are endangered, but you know, since the commercial whaling ban came in, numbers of certain whale species, like humpbacks, have hugely recovered. When we put our minds to it and come together, humans have the power to turn these things around ..."

At the word "humpbacks", the bedroom door flew open and Jesse ran across the room and threw himself into his mum's lap. "Tell me whale stories," he said, blinking up at her.

"We'll talk later," Mum whispered, and Finn nodded, relieved at the interruption.

"No, talk now!" demanded Jesse.

"Well," said Mum, stroking Jesse's hair, "did you know that whales are not *only* **beautiful** and **highly intelligent** creatures, but they're also saving the planet?"

"No," said Jesse, shoving his thumb in his mouth, "tell me."

"So the wonderful thing about whales is" – she leant down closer to Jesse and whispered into his ear – "they have **magic POO!**"

Jesse dissolved into giggles at the word, and even Finn couldn't help smiling.

"Now this poo is FULL of **nutrients** that makes these little microscopic plants that live in the ocean called phytoplankton multiply madly ... and the wonderful thing about phytoplankton is, not only do they **absorb tonnes and**

tonnes of harmful carbon from the atmosphere, but over millions of years they have also produced **over half of the oxygen** that we breathe today, can you believe that?"

Finn walked through to the kitchen and popped some bread in the toaster. He had heard these whale facts a million times, and so had Jesse, but Jesse still couldn't get enough of them. Finn sometimes wished that he was six again so that he could believe in magic and miracles too.

From the other room, he could hear his mum telling Jesse how a whale is like a rainforest, how they purify the air and fertilise the seas.

Finn looked out of the kitchen window. The sky was **grey** and the sea was **grey** and it was filled with plastic that was killing everything in it, killing our best chance of saving ourselves. Finn had read somewhere that by 2050 there'd be more plastic in the sea than fish. How could his mum bear it? What was the point in trying to save **a world that was already doomed?**

Finn jumped as the toast popped up, slightly burnt. He scraped off the burnt bits as best he could and spread it with butter and jam and took it through on a tray.

"Another wonderful thing about whales is," Mum was saying, "even at the end of a long life of keeping our oceans and our atmosphere healthy and producing whale calves that go on to do the same, when they do eventually die" – she looked pointedly at Finn – "they're **STILL** saving us. Because when whales die, they sink to the bottom of the ocean, taking tonnes of carbon from the atmosphere down with them, where it stays locked up on the sea floor for hundreds of years. Not only that, but all kinds of deep-sea animals live off their carcasses."

"Not if they die on the sand with a stomach full of plastic," muttered Finn.

A wailing sound came from Jesse and Mum shot Finn a sharp look. But the look softened as soon as it landed. She reached for Finn's hand. "Well, **that's where WE come in**, love, isn't it?"

She looked up at him searchingly.

"If we all work together, **everyone just doing their bit**, then we can clean our seas and save these beautiful creatures. Aren't they worth the effort? Isn't it at least worth a try?"

Finn met her eyes. They shone with hope.

He couldn't bear to disappoint her.

He forced a smile. "Of course it is," he said, and he went back to his room and closed the door, leaving Mum and Jesse to their stories.

Chapter 4

Girl Again

The next morning, Finn woke to the sound of seagulls **squawking**. The noise was so loud he thought for a moment one must be in the room. He pushed open the little window by his bed and leant out. Craning his head, he saw a flock of gulls circling high above the dunes. He breathed in a **great lungful of salty air**. It smelt fresh and lively, but the sky was still **endlessly, hopelessly grey**.

Leaving Jesse asleep, Finn tiptoed out into the hall.

There was a note from his mum on the dining room table.

See you at teatime. If you go to the beach, don't go far. Jim's coming at 1 p.m. Call me if you need me. Have fun!

Below it she had written out a series of phone numbers, including her own (as if they didn't already have it) and her colleague Aisha's who would also be on the boat with her, and Jim's, and the number of the whale and dolphin centre where Jim and Aisha worked, just in case.

Finn rolled his eyes and padded sleepily through to the kitchen, wondering what time she'd left. By now she was probably halfway out to sea, eyes fixed on the empty horizon, ever hopeful of spotting Arrow and the others.

Finn made toast and ate it standing in the kitchen as he scrolled through his phone. He could feel his mood growing **heavier and heavier** as he waded through endless sunny summer holiday posts from his friends – grinning in sunglasses, running along sunny beaches, lounging by pools – so it was almost a relief when Jesse burst into the kitchen and demanded that they go and look for whales like Finn had promised.

Outside it was fresher and brighter than it had looked through the window. The sun was doing its best to struggle through the clouds, but it was still bitterly cold for July.

"Where do you think the **humpback whales** are?" asked Jesse as he stomped down the gravel pathway.

"I'm not sure we'll be able to see whales from the land, Jess," said Finn gently.

"I think they're more out at sea. We might see dolphins though?"

Jesse stopped and frowned up at Finn.

"But we should definitely look, just in case," said Finn, backtracking. "I know – why don't we turn right when we hit the beach, then we're heading *towards* the sea."

Jesse nodded and marched on ahead, clearly satisfied with this response, and Finn traipsed along behind him. He rubbed his arms against the cold and wondered if they should have brought their raincoats.

There was a beep from his pocket and he pulled his phone out.

Hey, how's Scotland? Check this out! Wish u were here bro!

Finn seethed as he watched a video

of his friend Chris dive-bombing into a **luminous blue** *swimming* **pool**. Chris's brother must have filmed it, thought Finn. You could hear him laughing in the background.

A wave of furious anger surged through Finn, and for a second he felt like **hurling** his phone into the sea. Instead, he took a deep breath and put his phone on silent and shoved it back into his pocket. But the day felt **ruined**. The sky was **grey** and the sea was **grey** and on the sand at his feet was a discarded plastic bottle and Finn **kicked** at it mercilessly, booting it down the beach.

A familiar voice rang out from somewhere behind him.

"Are you going to pick that up or just kick it about?"

He spun round. At first he couldn't see anyone. Then he spotted her. It was the messy-haired girl from yesterday. She was sitting on a bench beneath some trees set back from the beach, her shaggy brown dog curled up asleep at her feet. In her hands, she held the pair of binoculars Finn had spotted the day before, which she'd clearly lowered for the express purpose of scowling at him.

"You tourists are **all the same,**" she said. "First one person drops it, then *they* just step right over it" – she nodded towards a family in the distance – "as if they don't even *see* it! Then *you* rock up and play football with it! **Don't you have bins** in whatever city you come from?"

She scowled at him a moment longer, then took up her binoculars again and stared straight past him, out to sea.

Finn felt his face flush red, first with shame, then with anger. He picked up the bottle. He was going to pick it up *anyway*. He only kicked it once. And where did she get off calling him a TOURIST? Did she even know why they were there, all the pointless sacrifices they were already making?

"We're not TOURISTS for your information," he said, brandishing the bottle at her. "My mum *works* here, **saving whales**. In *fact*," he went on, remembering Jim's parting words, "we're even going to a beach clean next week."

The girl lowered her binoculars a moment and eyed him coolly. "Aye grand," she said, raising them again. "City types come to save us."

Then she went right back to ignoring him.

Finn's blood boiled. "And anyway, if you really think **one bottle** is going to make a difference when the whole sea is already full of plastic then you're even stupider than you look!"

And without waiting for her reply, he stormed off down the beach, slam-dunking the bottle in the nearest recycling bin with probably a little more force than was strictly necessary.

Honestly, who did she think she was, lecturing him?

"Who was that girl?" asked Jesse.

"No one."

"Did she have a dog?"

"I don't know, come on ..." said Finn

taking his hand, "let's go and find whales."

"OK!" said Jesse, jogging to keep up with him. "I think they're this way ..." and Finn pretended to look too, but all he could see as they walked along the sand were his own angry thoughts. He was so cross that he didn't notice the sky turning a deep purply grey until they'd already been walking for some time.

"We'd better head back," he said, looking up as he felt the first fat drop fall.

Then from all around there was a deep rumble – and the skies opened.

The beach was already deserted as they raced back down it, all the beachgoers having magically disappeared as one, retreating to safety.

Jesse threw his arms out either side of

him, like a plane, as he had done the day before. "We're swimming like the whales!" he shouted, and suddenly Finn realised Jesse's arms **weren't** the wings of a plane; they were the giant, pectoral fins of a humpback. Finn laughed, feeling his mood lift as the adrenaline coursed through him and the wind raced past him and the **cool rain** fell on to his upturned face.

"Nearly there now!" he shouted between pants, though in truth he had no idea where they were because his glasses were covered in rain. Then from up ahead, he heard a dog barking and saw a blur of shaggy brown fur rising to attention at the back of the beach, and he realised where he must be.

"Hello, doggie!" said Jesse, running towards the dog.

"NO, Jesse!" shouted Finn, but it was too late. Jesse was already up there. He ran straight for the bench and sat down next to the girl, thrusting his fingers deep into the dog's fur.

"Hello, I'm Jesse," he said, looking up at her. "I like your dog. Do you know where any humpback whales are?"

"Jesse, come ON ..." shouted Finn. The last thing he wanted was to have to sit and make conversation with that **horrible** girl. He pushed the wet hair back off his face and dried his glasses on his T-shirt, aware of what a mess he must have looked when the girl was still sitting exactly where she had been, smug and dry beneath the trees.

"No, but there's a **pod of bottlenose dolphins** just out there

in the firth," said the girl, ignoring Finn
completely. "Would you like to see?"

"Yes, I would," said Jesse after
a moment. "My favourite are humpback
whales, but I do like dolphins too."

"Jesse, please, we need to get back ..."
said Finn desperately. The rain was slowing

now, but he was still getting **soaked**.

"Please can we stay, Finn, **PLEASE ...**"
begged Jesse. "I want to see the dolphins!"

The girl looked at Finn.

"Finn?" She raised an eyebrow.
"Is that your name?"

Finn was trying to work out how to reply
to this when she added, "Your family really
DO like whales, don't they?"

A tiny smile tugged at the corner of
Finn's mouth.

The girl eyed him a second longer, then
reached down to pull something out of her
bag. "I have a beach towel if you want to
borrow it ...?" And she held it out to him,
like a peace offering.

Finn walked up to the bench and took
the towel from her, muttering a thanks.

He dried his hair and rubbed at his arms. It didn't do much, but it was good to be out of the rain at least. He passed the towel to Jesse and sat down on the bench.

As Jesse dried his hair, Finn said quietly to the girl, "I *was* going to pick the bottle up, you know."

The girl flicked a look at him, then nodded. "OK, let's forget it then," she said lightly. After a moment she added, "Did you really mean what you said though?"

"Which bit?"

"About nothing making a difference?"

Finn shrugged. "How can it?" he said, kicking the sand. "There's too much that's already ruined ..."

"I don't know," the girl said. "I think **everything makes a difference**, even if it's only a little difference. Every time I **bring my own water bottle** to the beach or **pick up someone else's rubbish**, I think *that's an animal's life I just saved.*"

Finn thought about this for a moment. "Yes, but all the bad stuff everyone else does makes a difference *too*," said Finn, "and it cancels out the good stuff."

"Well, I can't do anything about what other people do," she said. "Only what *I* do."

"There you go, doggie!" said Jesse, who had finished drying himself and was now drying the dog, talking to it in a quiet voice as he rubbed it all over with the girl's towel. The dog was rolling around on its back, panting happily.

"Sorry about the towel," said Finn.

The girl chuckled. "Nae bother."

"What's his name?" asked Finn.

"She's a she," said the girl, "and she's called **Rain**."

Finn smiled. "That's a funny name for—"

"It was my mum's middle name," said the girl, looking at the sea through her binoculars again.

Finn noticed the "was". "Oh," he said, unsure what to say next. "Right. Is she ...?"

"Aye, she's dead," said the girl, finishing his sentence.

For the third time in less than twenty-four hours, Finn felt himself turn bright red in front of her.

"I'm sorry, I" – he looked down at his feet – "well, I know it's ... it's not the same, but our dad's not around either."

Jesse looked up. "He's not dead,

though," he said, matter-of-factly.
"He just left."

The girl lowered her binoculars. "Oh
aye? Well, I guess that's almost worse" –
she looked across at Finn – "in a way?"

Finn looked back at the girl, then
without really understanding why, they
both **burst** out laughing, a **great big
belly laugh**, the kind that gives you a
stitch in your side. They didn't laugh for
long, because it wasn't really funny, but it
felt good to let it out, whatever it was, like
the way the air feels clearer after the rain.
Then, just as they were stopping, they
noticed Jesse's frowning face looking
between them, trying to work out what the
joke was, and it set them off again.

"Sorry, Jesse," said Finn, at last getting
the laugh under control. "It's not funny,

I know." Jesse kept looking between them.
Then after a moment, he said, "Can I see
the dolphins now, please?"

Chapter 5

Dolphins

There's a feeling, like a bubble, that rises up in a person at the sight of a dolphin or a whale leaping out of the sea.

It's as if the heart **leaps** along with them, rejoicing at the amazing luck of catching a glimpse of a creature from another world briefly crossing over into ours.

"DOLPHINSSSSS!!!!!!" shouted Jesse, hopping excitedly from one foot to the other.

"Let me see, let me see," said Finn, standing and reaching for the binoculars, as excited as a six-year-old himself.

There were five or maybe even six of them. Their slick grey bodies shone and **sparkled** as one after the other they leapt right up out of the water, then dived back down again.

Finn passed the binoculars back to Jesse's grasping, outstretched hands and smiled at the girl as he sat again. "They're amazing," he said.

"Aye," she said. "But you're here for the whales?"

"Our mum is, yes," he said.

"She's a marine biologist."

The girl looked across at him, alert suddenly. "Oh aye?"

"She's researching minke whales."

"Humpbacks are *my* favourite though," said Jesse interrupting, "even though they're not as big as blue whales which are the biggest creatures on the **planet**, but humpbacks have the biggest pectoral fins, which are the ones on the side, and they have these HUGE tails, which means they can swim really fast and jump really, really high out of the water, which is called **breaching**. Finny and me are going to find one even though mostly there are minke whales in

Scopland, but you DO get humpbacks too."

"I know you do," said the girl. "I've seen one."

Jesse's eyes grew **wide *as* plates.** "Where?"

"I'll take you there. I know a good lookout spot."

Jesse stood up.

"Not *now*," said the girl.

Jesse frowned and sat down again. "When?"

Just then a voice called out from behind the trees. "Skye ...?"

The girl groaned. "That'll be my dad. Over here, Dad!"

"*Sky?*" said Finn. He smiled and raised his eyebrow at her. "Is that really your name?"

"Aye, Skye with an 'e'," explained Skye.

"It's a Scottish island."

"Skye and Rain?" said Finn, eyebrow still raised.

"Aye, well," – she motioned towards the cloud-filled sky – "you can see why!"

Finn laughed. "And you make fun of MY name ..."

"I don't know why you don't take your phone with you ..." said a man appearing through the trees.

"So that you can't hassle me," muttered

Skye under her breath.

"What's that, hen?" said the man. "Oh hello," he added when he saw Finn and Jesse.

Jesse walked right up to him. "Hello, I'm Jesse. Skye with an 'e' is going to show us where the humpback whales are."

The man laughed. "Is she now? Well, that'll have to be another day, pet, since it's gone lunchtime already and *someone* was supposed to be home half an hour ago."

"Oh no," said Finn standing abruptly, "What time is it?"

"It's half one," said the man.

"We have to go, Jesse," said Finn, pulling out his phone. There were three missed calls from Jim. "We're really late already."

"But **what about the humpbacks?"** wailed Jesse.

"I'll meet you here tomorrow at ten," said the girl, "or the next day if it's raining."

"Deal," said Finn.

"Deal!" said Jesse.

"Well, that's that sorted then," said the girl's dad with a smile. "Bye, boys, nice to meet you!"

***

Finn and Jesse ran all the way back to the house. Jim was outside, waiting in his car.

"I was beginning to think it was something I'd said!" he joked, getting out. "Now – who wants to see some **dolphins?"**

"No thank you," said Jesse before Finn

could stop him, "we've just seen some."

Jim blinked. "Oh, right."

"Do you know where any humpback whales are though?"

"Sorry," said Finn. "He's obsessed."

Jim smiled. "And who can blame him! They're only one of the mightiest creatures in the ocean ..."

"And you DO get them in Scopland," said Jesse, seriously.

"Oh aye," agreed Jim. "It's rare to see them from the land, but it's not unheard of. Well, I **can't guarantee** seeing any real-live humpback whales *today*, but would you like to hop in the car with me and go to the centre where I could show you our collection of whale bones?"

Jesse thought for a moment. "Yes, I would," he said with a nod, and he got into

Jim's car and slammed the door, at which
point Finn promptly opened it again and
got him out so they could get changed
into some dry clothes first.

It was a perfect afternoon for Jesse.
By the time Jim dropped them back at the
house later, he was **fizzing** with new
facts to tell Mum: about whales and whale
bones, and about Skye with an 'e', and the
shaggy brown dog, and the dolphins.

"That's nice, love," said Mum, but Finn
thought she seemed a little distracted,
and when he asked if she'd seen Arrow
or any of the others, she just said, "Hmm?"
as if she hadn't heard and then changed
the subject, which wasn't like her at all.
Nor was it like her to agree so quickly
when Finn asked if they could spend the
day with their new friend Skye tomorrow

rather than trouble Jim again, which she said was fine as long as they let Jim know.

Perhaps she's just tired, Finn thought as he got ready for bed, but whatever the reason, Finn wasn't going to complain.

They had an adventure to go on tomorrow, and to his surprise, Finn realised he couldn't wait.

Chapter 6

A Little Yellow Dinghy

The weather, unfortunately, had **other ideas**.

When Finn woke the next morning it was to the sound of rain **pounding** against his bedside window. It rained all morning, and though it stopped for a brief while in the afternoon, it then proceeded to rain all evening, all night, and all the next day too.

In fact, it rained almost **constantly** for two entire days.

Finn paced the wooden floorboards of the little cottage like an animal in a zoo. He moved from room to room, playing

77

restlessly with his phone, but he couldn't settle. He longed to be back outside again.

Jesse was no better. He sat mournfully at a chair by the window, asking every half an hour when the rain would stop, as if Finn might somehow know.

Jim came like clockwork each lunchtime to keep them company and bring them food, even though Finn was perfectly capable of making his own lunch, as he grumbled to himself. But Jim was friendly and kind and he helped keep Jesse distracted with whale stories for a few hours of the day, so Finn told himself not to complain.

When at last on the third morning Finn woke to clear skies, he **leapt** out of bed like it was his birthday.

Mum had left a note on the table again, and a packed lunch.

Hope the weather holds! Have fun with your friend. Made you some sandwiches. Don't go far, and stay in touch with Jim and me.

"Come on, Jesse, time to get up!" Finn called, and he stuffed a backpack with raincoats and sandwiches and water and snacks and by 9.45 a.m. they were both dressed and out the door. Sure enough, when they reached the bench beneath the trees, there was Skye, waiting.

"Hello, Skye with an 'e'!" said Jesse. "And hello, doggie!"

Rain barked and bounded towards her new friend, her tail wagging excitedly, and Jesse knelt down in the sand to cuddle her. He tumbled backwards in a **fit of giggles** as she planted a great big lick all the way up his cheek.

"I thought the rain would never stop!" said Finn, grinning.

"Call that rain?" said Skye. She rolled her eyes. "You city types ... Now come on, this way!" and she led them on down the beach.

They walked along the sand for hours. The sun kept coming  out, then dipping behind clouds, then coming out again, one minute making the sea shine with **dancing sunlight**, the next casting it into shade, throwing down fast-moving cloud shadows on to the sand that would pass over them and on down the beach. The beach seemed to go on forever, just sand and sea as far as the eye could see, though if you really squinted you could see that at some point in the distance the sand ended in rocks, and the rocks rose up into cliffs.

Sometimes Skye would lead them into the grassy dunes or the trees that lined the back of the beach, and at one point a river cut right across the sand on its way out into the firth, and they had to follow it upstream and cross over a little wooden bridge to get to the other side. At moments along the way, Skye would stop suddenly, duck down, and say *shhhhh*, and show them where to point the binoculars. She pointed out **wagtails and sandpipers,**

kestrels and kittiwakes, otters and ospreys, and soon even Jesse was so captivated that for a moment he forgot about whales completely.

When they at last approached the final curve of the beach where the sand ended abruptly at the rocks, Skye called out to Rain and put her on the lead. A moment later Finn understood why. A noise of delight escaped him. There on the sand, stretched out on the sand beneath the rocks, was a **colony of harbour seals**, their fat speckled bodies basking lazily in the sun.

Skye pointed out a newborn seal pup, who was snuggled into the warmth of its mum. Another mother-and-pup pair were rubbing noses as they looked lovingly at each other, their eyes huge and dark and

soulful. The bond between them looked so *human*, thought Finn, and he was about to say this when he suddenly remembered that Skye didn't have a mum any more, and to his surprise, he felt such a wave of sadness for his new friend that tears pricked the back of his eyes.

"You OK?" said Skye, eyeing him strangely.

"Oh yes, fine," said Finn, rubbing his eyes. "Hay fever, I think."

"Can I stroke one?" Jesse whispered, walking slowly in the direction of the seals with a hand outstretched, and Skye said casually, "As long as you don't mind **losing a finger.**"

Jesse snapped his arm back to his side and slowly retreated.

"Do they really bite?" asked Finn, surprised.

"Aye, especially round pupping season," she said. "Seals are very protective of their young, so best to stay away. Besides, they don't really like being stroked, so that kind of takes the fun out of it."

Jesse kept his distance after that and they all gave the seals a wide birth as Skye led them towards the rocks at the end of the beach. Finn was just wondering when she was going to turn around as it didn't look like there was a way through here, only back the way they'd come, when to his surprise she leapt up on to the rocks like a mountain goat.

Finn and Jesse blinked up at her.

"Um," said Finn, "are you sure?"

Skye looked down at them, hands on hips. "Well, do you want to see the whales or not?" And with that she began scrambling over the rocks, only pausing to shout over her shoulder, "It's not far. There's a path on the other side once you get over the top."

"Fine!" Finn shouted after her, not wanting to be outdone. "Well, why didn't you just say so in the first place!" and he turned to Jesse to see if he wanted a piggyback, but Jesse was already on the rocks.

"Come on, Finny!" he said. "We're off to see the whales!"

The rocks were a little slippery at first, but they had plenty of hand- and footholds, and Finn soon found it was quite easy once you'd got the hang of it.

It wasn't long before they were at the top
and could see over the rocky outcrop to
what lay on the other side.

Finn had been expecting to see another
sandy bay, backed by the high cliffs they
could see from the beach, but in fact, laid
out below them was a harbour. **Fishing
boats of all different sizes and
colours** were bobbing about as boats
do, buffeted by winds and waves.

"That little yellow one is ours," said
Skye, when they'd caught up with her.

A thought occurred to Finn.
"Can I borrow your binoculars?" he asked,
directing them out towards the Outer
Moray, and the sea. From this height, he
might just be able to see ... "There it is!"
he shouted. "Look, Jesse, that must be
Mum ..." and he pointed to a big boat

with the whale and dolphin centre logo on its side.

"I wish I was out there," said Skye wistfully.

"Don't you go out on your boat?" asked Finn.

"Not since Mum died," said Skye, walking on towards a path that veered sharply up the cliff.

"Did your mum drown?" asked Jesse, looking up at her, and Finn said, "Jesse!" but Skye just laughed.

"No, she had cancer," she said, her laugh dying with the word, "but the boat was more her thing than Dad's. Now he says the boat just reminds him of her, but in truth, he never had sea legs. He's always preferred the shore, **collecting and making stuff**, that's what he loves."

"What sort of stuff?" asked Finn.

"Blue stuff mostly." Smiling at Finn's confused expression, she stopped and pulled out a **necklace** from under her T-shirt. "Like this ..." she said, showing them a string of brightly coloured blue beads, all different shades, all plastic.

"He makes all kinds of stuff out of it ... mosaics and picture frames and postcards. Sells them in the tourist shops," she said, walking off again. "Does all right out of it too."

The path climbed up and up. "Not far now," said Skye over her shoulder. "No looking till we get to the top!"

It seemed to be getting **mistier** as they climbed, as if they were climbing right up into the clouds, and the air felt cooler too, but perhaps the weather was

just changing again, thought Finn. It was
hard to tell, since they weren't allowed
to look at anything, but glancing up at
the sky, Finn couldn't help but notice
that the patches of blue from earlier had
disappeared, covered over by a thick
layer of low-hanging cloud.

"Here we are!" said Skye, as she
reached the top. "On a clear day from
up here, you can see all the way back
to Inverness and all the way out to ..."

Her voice trailed away and she gasped.
Below them was a **sea of fog**.

"You can barely even see the harbour,"
she breathed. She put a hand on Jesse's
shoulder, and looking down at him she
said, "I'm sorry, Jesse, I don't think we're
going to see any whales today."

For a moment, it looked like Jesse

was going to start crying, then his
face changed.

"Is that ... **barking?"**

They all listened. Then they heard it.
It sounded muffled and echoey, like it
was coming from miles below. But it had
an edge to it too – *a warning*, or a cry
for help.

"Sounds like she's at the cove," said
Skye. "She sounds scared ... come on."

So they ran on along the cliff path,
treading as carefully as they could
because by now the fog was so thick they
could hardly see their feet in front of them
as the path began to descend steeply
down and down towards the tiny half-
moon bay below.

Skye was calling out to Rain all the way,
but it wasn't until they got to the last step

that they saw her.

"What is it, girl?" said Skye, bending to stroke her and put her on the lead again. She was crouched at the back of the beach, hackles up, whimpering in terror at **something** at the water's edge, *a dark shape in the shallows*.

And then they realised what it was.

Chapter 7

Stranded

Finn's stomach plummeted, like a broken lift, and for a moment he thought he might be sick.

It was a whale. **A young minke whale**, Finn realised from the size and shape of it, a juvenile, like the one in the Thames. And he was stranded, beached on the sand of this tiny, half-moon cove. The shallows were still lapping back and forth beneath him, but the greater part of his skin was exposed to the elements.

Though the whale was young, he was still huge – four or five metres long at least – **bigger than a car,** and just as out of place on the sand. It just looked wrong, sickening.

Finn was struck dumb; stupefied by shock. Then the sound of Jesse crying brought him back round.

Finn span round and took Jesse by the shoulders, crouching down so their eyes were level. "Everything's going to be all right, OK? Do you believe me?" Jesse nodded slowly, but he kept peering round Finn to where the whale lay stranded on the sand.

"Don't worry, we'll sort this ..." said Finn. "The tide must be coming in by now, right, Skye?"

Skye's mouth was opening and closing, like a fish, but no sounds were coming out.

"Skye?"

She turned to Finn, snapping out of her

trance. Finn could see her slowly taking in his question. She shook her head, her eyes full of fear. "Not for another two hours at least ..."

Finn cursed and Jesse started crying again.

"How long can they survive out of water?" asked Skye.

The truth was, Finn didn't know the answer. He knew that whales breathed the air, like humans – that's what their blowholes were for. But he also knew that the sea kept them cool, supported their vast weight, that after a while on land, their skin would get dry and they'd overheat and ...

"Finn?" Skye was looking at him.

"I think he'll be OK for a while," he said, not wanting to worry Jesse more. "But we

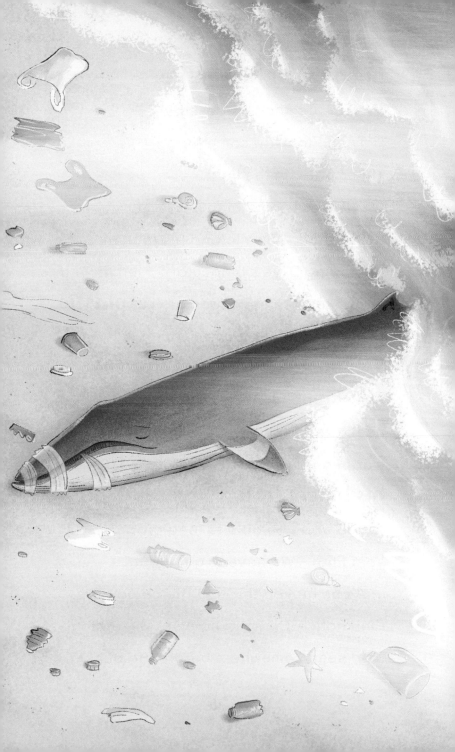

need to get him in the water as soon as possible."

Then Finn saw something shimmering in the light.

"He's got something in his mouth ..." Swallowing his fear, and borrowing Skye's binoculars, Finn moved a few steps closer. It was a bit of **plastic sheeting**, a long, thin strip of it. It was the sort of material a box might once have been wrapped in, but now it had wrapped itself around the whale's head. It was trapped in his mouth, in the **bristles of his baleen**.

"He won't be able to feed properly," said Finn. "We have to get it out."

As he looked through the binoculars, Finn noticed something else, something he'd seen somewhere before. He blinked in disbelief at the distinctive, triangular-shaped scar on the whale's dorsal fin.

"Oh my gosh," he breathed, **"it's Arrow."**

He spun around. "Mum was looking for this whale ... he's been missing." Finn rummaged in his bag. "We'll call her!" he said, pulling his phone out. "She'll come on the boat!" But when he looked at his phone his heart fell. "No reception." He looked at Skye, panic on his face. "You don't have ...?"

Skye winced and shook her head. "Sorry," she said. "I never bring it ... Let's run back up to the lookout point – we're sure to get reception up there."

"But we can't just leave him!" wailed Jesse.

"We have to, Jess ..." said Finn.

"We have to get help. Come on ... Mum will know what to do."

But when they reached the top again, panting and out of breath, there was still no reception. Finn kicked at the ground in frustration.

"What do we do?" asked Skye.

Finn racked his brains. "Should we go to the centre?"

"It's hours from here," said Skye, "and anyway, the rescue boat is out there!"

"How long to your place? We could get your phone?"

"It's up near yours ... a two-hour walk at least."

"What about a phone box?"

"Porthead's is probably the closest, but it's still miles away. It's nothing but boats round here."

The word **"boats"** hung in the misty air between them.

Finn and Skye looked at each other, and in the look a crazy plan took shape.

Chapter 8

Lost At Sea

"This one?" said Finn.

A **little yellow dinghy** creaked and swayed on its mooring in front of them. Its paintwork was the colour of sunflowers, but it was chipped and flaking, and the boat looked like it hadn't been used in a long time.

"Aye," said Skye, a defensive note in her voice.

"This is your fishing boat?" He turned to Skye, eyebrow raised.

All around them were sturdy-looking vessels, with glass wheelhouses and big steering wheels, some with stairs leading down to little cabins below deck. The boat in front of them was tiny, with a tiller and a little engine and two oars.

Skye snapped her head round. "Well, do *you* have a boat we can use?" she said, scowling at him.

"Me?" said Finn innocently. **"I'm** just a **city boy,** remember? **You're** the one from the fishing village."

"Well, Mum was vegetarian," said Skye defensively. "We only ever took it out for fun."

Rain was barking excitedly at the boat. "Come on, doggie, let's go and save the whale!" said Jesse, and without waiting for the others, he and Rain jumped aboard and went and sat in the bow.

Finn sighed. "And you're sure you know how to drive it?"

"Oh aye," said Skye, but there was a **quiver** of doubt in her voice. "I mean, I've seen Mum and Dad do it a million times." She sounded like she was trying to persuade herself.

Finn stared at her. "So you've never actually done it yourself?"

"I've steered plenty," she said. "I've just never *started* it myself. But I know how to do it." She looked down at the engine. "I think."

"Right," said Finn, not feeling very reassured.

"Let me get it going," said Skye, "then you can cast off and jump in."

"Um, cast off?" asked Finn.

Skye smirked. "Haven't you ever been on a boat before?"

"I have, but only big ones," said Finn in

as dignified a voice as he could manage.

Skye rolled her eyes. "Cast off means undo the rope that's tying the boat to the jetty. Just try not to fall in, city boy."

For a long while, it seemed like the boat wouldn't start. Skye tugged at the starter chain, once, twice, three times. Each time it spluttered, then died.

"Maybe it's out of petrol," she said, but on the fourth try **the engine roared to life**.

"Yes!" shouted Skye, and Finn untied the boat and leapt aboard. A moment later they were all whooping and cheering as the little boat chugged out of the misty harbour.

But as soon as they left the harbour walls, the cheering stopped. Out of the protection of the land, the sea changed.

It became rough and choppy, the wind whipping it up into a frenzy. **Waves bashed against the bow** and the little boat rocked dangerously from side to side.

"We won't drown, will we?" said Jesse, looking back at Finn. He was clinging tightly to Rain, his fingers gripping her fur.

"Of course we won't," said Finn, with much more confidence than he felt. He looked across at Skye and noticed that the hand on the tiller was shaking. "You can do this," he said, putting a hand on her shoulder, and Skye nodded, eyes fixed on the sea ahead.

"Can you see your mum's boat?" she asked, squinting through the mist.

But Finn couldn't see anything. The fog seemed to have **closed in around**

them. It was like sailing through a cloud.

"Let me try with the binoculars," he said, but as he reached over to take them from Skye **a huge wave smashed into them**, spraying water over the side of the boat, and he lost his balance.

"NO!" shouted Skye as **the binoculars slipped** from Finn's grasp into the foaming sea.

Finn cursed internally. "I'm sorry," he said.

"It's OK," said Skye, but Finn could tell she was upset.

"Just keep going the way you're going," he said. "You were headed in the right direction, I'm sure."

But the truth was, he had no idea; he couldn't see a thing.

They moved through the fog in worried silence – three children and a dog, alone and lost at sea.

And then, quite suddenly, they weren't alone.

First came the fish. Rain barked and barked as one after another **a parade of shiny, silver-blue mackerel** leapt out of the churning water kicked up by the bow. Jesse laughed and pointed as

Rain barked and snapped and tried to catch one in her teeth.

Then came the seabirds. Cawing and squawking, they swooped down from the clouds to hover above the boat, then **dropped like stones**, diving for the mackerel. One or two got lucky and flew away with their catch in their beaks while the others fell into an easy formation around the boat, like sentries.

Then came the dolphins. Finn spotted one first, then Jesse saw one on the other side, and another too, and to their delight they soon realised that the boat was surrounded, a friendly pod **leaping and swimming and chattering** alongside them, not a metre from the boat.

In fact, they had almost forgotten about the rescue boat completely, when Skye shouted, "There it is!"

Finn ran to the bow and whooped as at last the big boat came into view, swaying and creaking within its cloak of fog. Finn and Jesse both **screamed** at the tops of their voices – **"MUM!"**

But the wind seemed to whip their cries away.

"Let's try again," said Finn to Jesse. "On three? One ... two ... "

"MUM!"

And this time someone did hear.

A figure turned towards them, running to the side of the boat for a closer look. Then they disappeared and came back with someone else.

"MUM!" Jesse and Finn called again, and they jumped and waved their arms around.

And sure enough, it was Mum. She peered through the fog, blinking in astonishment at the strange and unforgettable sight of her two sons, a girl and a dog on a little yellow dinghy powering across the water towards her.

Chapter 9

Rescue Operation

The children and the dog were helped aboard by a **bewildered** Mum and her two colleagues, and the little boat was secured to the big one.

After some hasty introductions and explanations, Finn described what they'd found – **the beached whale, the plastic round its head, the arrow-shaped scar** on its fin.

And though part of Mum was furious with Finn for taking such a risk, this was clearly no time for recriminations. "We'll talk about this later," said Mum, and at her nod, Aisha spun the boat around and they set off for the little cove.

At the mention of the arrow-shaped scar, Mum's face had looked grim, but not surprised. Finn remembered how quiet and distracted she'd been the other night.

"You knew," he said, working it out, "you'd seen him already."

Mum nodded. "We didn't know it was Arrow, but we'd seen a young whale moving strangely in the water a few days ago. We tried to follow him, but we lost him. We've been looking for him ever since."

"Will the whale be OK?" asked Skye, flicking anxious looks between Finn and his mum. Now they'd got over the adrenaline of the boat ride, *a fear as thick as the fog* was settling around them.

"I'm afraid there's no way of knowing yet," said Mum. "But we'll do everything we can for him, I promise."

The knot in Finn's stomach **tensed and twisted** as they rounded the bend on the other side of the cliffs and turned in towards the half-moon bay. A heavy silence fell over the boat as they saw the whale. It was now completely out of the water.

News travels fast in a small community and since they'd left, a little crowd of locals had gathered on the sand.

"Oh no," said Skye, spotting her dad among them. "I'm for it, now ..."

But as the big boat's engine was turned off and the children were rowed ashore in the dinghy, along with equipment from the rescue boat, it was clear that no one was in trouble.

Skye's dad hugged her to him fiercely. "Don't scare me like that again!" he said, and he led the children away to where the locals were waiting with thermos flasks of hot drinks and packets of biscuits. But Skye and Finn couldn't settle, and passing Rain's lead to Jesse, they soon gravitated back to the water's edge to watch as the team from the rescue boat got to work.

First, **ever so carefully**, they removed the plastic from Arrow's mouth.

Next, using buckets from the rescue boat, they poured seawater over his skin, to keep him cool and wet, as whales like to be, taking care to avoid his blowhole.

Then came the tricky bit. An inflatable raft had to be fed beneath the whale's middle, then inflated, to help the whale to keep himself upright and support his **huge** weight. The raft was then attached to the rescue boat with a long rope.

The whole time, the team talked quietly to the whale in soft and soothing tones, trying to let him know that they were there to help, that they wouldn't hurt him.

Skye and Finn hovered anxiously nearby. "Will you tow him out on the raft?" Skye asked Mum as she walked towards them.

Mum shook her head. "He's too heavy," she explained. "There's nothing we can do until the tide comes back in. Once he's afloat again, we'll see what we can do. In the meantime, we just have to keep him comfortable, and **wait**, and hope he'll

be strong enough to swim away when the time comes."

She gave Skye and Finn a smile and put a hand on each of their shoulders. "It won't be long now. Go and get a mug of cocoa and a biscuit – you've done all you can."

Finn and Skye nodded and reluctantly dropped back. As they walked away, Skye shook her head and said, "Wow, your mum is amazing." Her voice was full of awe, and for the first time, Finn realised it was true. "Yeah, I know," he said, and he felt his chest swell with pride.

They went over to where Jesse was sitting, snuggled into Rain's shaggy brown coat.

"Don't worry," Jesse was saying to Rain as he fed her biscuits, "everything will be all right, OK?"

Finn and Skye shared a smile as they sat either side of him, Finn's hand on Jesse's head, Skye's fingers knotted into Rain's fur.

And like that they **waited,** and they **watched,** as slowly, surely

the tide began to creep back up the beach.

It wasn't long before the whale was afloat once more.

The crowd **cheered** as at last they saw Arrow lift off the sand, but Mum turned to them and in a loud whisper asked them **to please be quiet.**

"This whale has been through a huge ordeal," she explained. "If he's too scared or too weak he may not be able to swim away ..."

So as the rescue boat gently towed the

raft and the now floating whale out into deeper water, and as the raft was deflated from around the whale and the boat moved **slowly, quietly away** from it, the crowd waited in hushed silence, **barely daring to breathe.**

Chapter 10

Away

And then quite suddenly, the whale pumped his tail and **off he flew through the water!**

The crowd **erupted**, then a moment later **gasped** as, in a single beautiful movement, the whale's body rose up out of the water, then plunged down again beneath the surface towards the deep, and disappeared out of sight.

Finn and Skye and Jesse all leapt up
and danced around in a circle, laughing
and cheering, and Rain barked and
barked, and jumped up at them, wanting
to be part of whatever was going on.

Mum walked up the beach to join them,
beaming from ear to ear, and Skye's
dad came over too.

"Hello," said Mum, putting out her hand
to him, "you must be Skye's dad. She's
a very brave girl driving that boat all
by herself."

"Aye," he said, shaking her hand, and
grinning broadly. "Brave like her mum,
stupid like her dad."

And as their parents chatted shyly to each other, and Jesse giggled and chased Rain around the beach, Finn and Skye sat down on the sand together, then fell backwards, laughing and looking up at the sky.

Finn could feel **a knot inside him loosen**. He turned his face to Skye. "Well done, Skye with an 'e'."

Skye smiled up into the clouds. "Aye, well done yourself," she said. "You were not bad" – she turned to him, a glint in her eye – "for a city boy."

Chapter 11

Every Bottle
Makes A Difference

As luck would have it, the day of the beach clean was the **sunniest day of the summer** yet.

And Jim was right – folks turned out in their droves.

The beach was **chock-full of locals**, who'd all come out to do their bit.

Everyone met at the whale and dolphin centre at nine, where bags to collect the rubbish in were handed out. The children's brave rescue of the minke whale was still on everyone's lips, and for the first half an hour of the day, there was much handshaking and backslapping as Mum and her boys were introduced to the locals, and everyone congratulated Skye and Finn and the team from the boat for their **brilliant work** in saving Arrow.

Then when everyone was ready, they set off from the centre, which was on the most westerly tip of the long, curving sandy bay, and slowly walked the length of the sand, past the cottage where Finn and Jesse and Mum were staying, past the bench under the trees where they'd first met Skye, and on towards the rocks where the seals were still happily snoozing in the sun.

The beach couldn't have looked more different to the other day.

The sky was a **bright and brilliant blue** and visibility was so good that even at its widest point you could see all the way to the other side of the firth. It was a perfect day for whale watching, so Skye promised Jesse that after the beach clean, she'd take them up to the lookout point again. But by the time they'd made it to the end of the beach where the seals were basking, Jesse was so tired, Finn had to give him a piggyback home.

It had been a long day, and they'd all learnt a lot. Mum's colleague Aisha from the boat had explained a bit more about plastic pollution – how it was not just the big stuff that was the problem, the stuff you could see, but also the little stuff called **"microplastics."**

"Did you know," she'd explained, "that

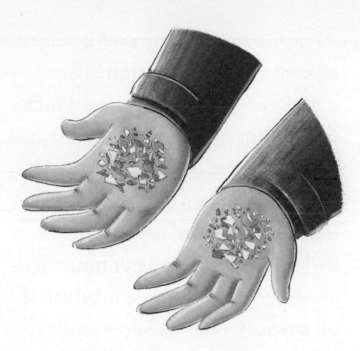

just a single one-litre plastic bottle can
break down into enough tiny pieces of
plastic to put a piece on **every single
mile of beach** on the planet?"

"Ha!" Skye had exclaimed, punching
Finn on the arm. "See? One bottle
does make a difference.
A HUGE difference."

And for once Finn had been pleased to admit that **she was right.**

By the end of the day, **twenty sacks of plastic** had been collected up by the beach-clean team. Finn didn't know what was more amazing – the fact that all that plastic had once been on the beach, or the fact that in **just a few hours**, just a few people had managed to **whisk it all away**, leaving the beach pristine once again. It was certainly a big haul for Skye's dad, who beeped and waved goodbye as he and Skye carted it all away in his little truck.

As Finn walked back along the now quiet beach, his mum just behind him chatting to a colleague, the sleepy weight of his little brother resting on his back, he felt a new feeling stirring inside him,

a tiny swirling whirlpool of ...
He didn't want to jinx it by putting a name
to it, but whatever it was, **it felt good**.
He looked out across the firth and smiled.
The sky was **blue** and the sea was
green and there was a **whole world**
down there inhabited by **beautiful,
underwater creatures** that were
worth saving, that were worth every tiny
sacrifice, because every sacrifice **really
did** make a difference.

Chapter 12

Spyhopping

The end of the summer came too soon, as it always did.

Finn couldn't work out where the six weeks had gone. It seemed to him like they'd only just arrived, and at the same time, that first day could have been a lifetime ago. So much had changed, in him, and around him. The world seemed to him a different place, full of **light** and

hope and **intrigue.**

The whale and dolphin centre had given Skye a **new pair of binoculars** to the replace the ones she'd lost overboard, and Finn and Jesse had been given a pair to  share too, and the rest of the summer had been spent with them glued to their eyes. Come rain or shine, they'd be out there, sitting on the rocks at the end of the beach, being careful not to disturb the seals, or if they had the energy and it was a clear enough day, they'd walk up to the lookout point.

Their hair had gone a few shades lighter and their skin a few shades darker, arms bronzed by the sun, cheeks pinked by the sea air. And though the knot in Finn's stomach hadn't completely disappeared, he had felt it slowly loosening more and more as the weeks had gone on.

"We should call ourselves something," Skye had said one day as they were sitting on the rocks above the harbour, and Finn had suggested **"the Whale Watchers"** and no one had bothered to think of anything else, because it was perfect.

Jesse as ever was on the lookout for humpbacks, though he hadn't seen one yet.

And of course, they were all hoping to spot Arrow.

Mum had explained to them that the only real way to know that a rescued whale had made it was if it was resighted. So on the last week of their holiday, when they still hadn't seen Arrow, and Mum's work for the summer was done, she offered to take them all out on the boat.

They waited for a clear day, when visibility was at its best. Skye's dad was invited too, but he politely declined.

"He's busy working on something," said Skye, but when Finn asked what she just smiled and said, "Something big," and she wouldn't say anything more.

The big boat **sliced** through the water, heading for where the Outer Moray met the North Sea. It felt very different to being on the little yellow dinghy, thought Finn. The centre's boat was sturdy, untroubled by the waves that bumped against it.

Finn noticed Skye kept darting little looks at his mum, as if she wanted to ask her something. Eventually, in a very casual voice, while looking studiously at her fingernails, she said, "So how did you start doing this for a job then?"

Mum shot her a smile. "By doing *exactly* what you're doing," she said. "Just looking and looking. Of course, there are courses you can do too, and exams, depending on what area you want to get into, but the *looking* is the key. And stay in touch with the guys at the centre. You always need a helping hand, don't you, Aisha?"

"Oh aye," said Aisha. "How about joining our whale and dolphin Shorewatch team, for a start? You've got the binoculars already ..."

Skye's eyes shone as she nodded and

said, "That'd be grand, thanks!"

"Come see me at the centre and I'll tell you all about it."

Once out at sea, Aisha turned the engine off, and everyone grew quiet as they all pointed their binoculars at the horizon.

Which was probably why they didn't notice the **dark shapes** approaching the boat from below the surface.

It was Skye who saw them first. "Over here!" she called, and the others dashed across to look.

There were three of them, all spyhopping around the boat, poking their little heads up to say hello.

"Well, they're definitely minkes!" said Jim.

One of the whales seemed particularly

curious. He came right up to the boat and seemed to eye them all with great intelligence. Finn's heart was **bouncing against his ribcage** as he bent down towards him.

"Hello there," he said, hoping to catch a glimpse of the tell-tale scar, but without even seeing it, he knew. **He could feel it** as he looked into the whale's eyes – this was Arrow, he was quite sure – and when the little whale finally swam away, breaching as he went, giving them all a perfect view of his arrow-shaped scar, it only confirmed what Finn had already known.

"Why are you crying, Finny?" asked Jesse, squinting across at him. "Aren't you happy?"

Finn adjusted his glasses and wiped at

his cheek. "I'm not crying," he said gruffly.

Skye eyed him carefully. "Hay fever again?" she said, and she raised an eyebrow.

Finn wiped at his face and shrugged, and they both started laughing.

Jesse looked back and forth between them, trying to work out the joke. Then he gave up. He picked up his binoculars again.

Everyone had seen what they wanted, but he *still* hadn't seen a humpback.

And now Aisha was starting up the engine, and the boat was turning around and heading back to the shore.

Jesse went and sat quietly at the back of the boat, binoculars fixed on the retreating sea behind.

It was such a clear day, if he only looked ...

And **looked** ...

And **looked** ...

A cry escaped from him, and everyone on the boat turned just in time to see it too. And they all cried out, their hearts **leaping** into their mouths as they saw ... first, a giant head, rising from the sea ... then a pair of huge pectoral fins, held out to the side like wings ... followed by the vast and unmistakable outline of *a humpback whale* as it hurled its body right up out of the water – twisted once in the air in an arc of sunlit sea spray – then crashed back down again to be swallowed whole by the sea, like it had never happened.

Jesse spun round to face the others, as if checking that they'd seen it too.

His whole face was transformed into a beaming, ear-to-ear grin.

And as the boat headed back to the shore and the sun melted into the sea turning everything pink, Finn wondered if this might have been the **best summer holiday** that anyone in the **whole history of summer holidays** had ever been lucky enough to go on.

Chapter 13

Blue Stuff

It was an early morning train, not a
sleeper, that would take them home, and
they'd arrive at dusk rather than dawn.
The holiday that was once just starting
was now at its end – the summer over,
a new school year soon to begin.

All these thoughts and more were
in Finn's mind as the train pulled away,
leaving the station platform – and the
holiday – behind them.

Finn and Jesse and Mum settled
themselves around their table, and Mum
got out their refillable water bottles,
and the sandwiches from her trusty

Tupperware tubs, as usual, but this time Finn didn't complain. He felt **proud of his mum** – proud that they were doing their bit – though he had to admit that he did feel a *little* bit jealous of the crisps that the family on the table across from them were opening.

Before Finn could stop him, Jesse walked over to their table.

"Hello, I'm Jesse," he said. "Do you know that all that plastic stuff ends up in the sea and it hurts whales and fish and birds, and whales are actually AMAZING, especially humpback whales, which are my favourite, and we just—"

"OK, love, that's enough," said Mum, ushering him back into his seat and shooting an apologetic look at the dads who were sitting across from them.

"No, no, he's quite right!" said one of them, chuckling. "And normally we do try, but we were a bit short on time this morning ... only just made the train! We'll try to remember next time, won't we, kids?"

And Finn smiled as the kids rolled their eyes, just like he used to.

The journey was long, and for most of it all three of them were quiet, even Jesse, which was a first. A sad, end-of-summer-holiday feeling had settled over them, like a cloud. Finn wished he had some photos to look back over, but he realised that for most of the big moments of the trip – finding Arrow, taking the boat out, the humpback whale breaching – he had been so caught up in the adventure, it hadn't even occurred to him to reach for his phone. He did have a few photos of him and Skye though, and of Jesse rolling around in the sand with Rain, and of the colony of harbour seals lying lazily in the sun.

Finn dozed for a while, then stared out of the window with his headphones on for what seemed like hours, then at some point he must have drifted off again because later when his phone pinged and he looked out of the window, he saw that the sky outside was growing dusky and the hills and fields had turned to houses and high-rises, which meant they must be nearing London.

He reached for his phone to check his

messages. There were two, one from his friend Chris, one from Skye.

He opened Chris's first.

You back yet? How was Scotland? Hope it didn't rain the whole time :)

Finn smiled and immediately started tapping away.

It was amazing! Loads of cool animals, like these seals ... We rescued a beached whale too, and collected 20 huge sacks of plastic off the beach!

Then he opened the message from Skye. It was a video message.

He exclaimed loudly as it started playing and Mum sat up in her seat and said, "What?" and Jesse said, "Lemme see, lemme see!"

Finn said, "One sec," and quickly forwarded the video on to Chris.

And look what my friend's dad made with all the plastic!

Then he put the video back to the beginning, and Mum and Jesse huddled round to watch it with him.

It was Skye and her dad, and they

were standing either side of **a giant sculpture**. It was a whale – bigger than both of them – and it was made entirely out of **tiny little bits of blue, all different shades, all plastic.**

Rain was jumping up at them and barking as usual, and Skye and her dad were grinning and waving at the camera.

"Come back and see us soon, **Whale Watchers!**" said Skye.

And Finn smiled, because he knew for a fact that one day soon, they would.

The End.

A note on the Moray Firth and the whale and dolphin centre

The landscape of this story is imaginary, made up of different bits of different places along the Moray Firth that have been taken apart and jumbled up and put back together in a way that suited the story.

But the Moray Firth itself is real, and there is a real dolphin centre there too, run by the wonderful charity Whale and Dolphin Conservation.

dolphincentre.whales.org

There is a resident population of bottlenose dolphins in the Moray Firth, and minke whales are known to live there too, as well as otters and ospreys, kittiwakes and kestrels, and many a harbour seal basking on the sand in the sun. And if you're lucky, and you look out to the North Sea, you might just spot a humpback whale.

There isn't a big blue whale sculpture made of plastic in the Moray Firth, but there IS one in Bruges, in Belgium. It's made of five tonnes of ocean plastic pulled out of the Atlantic and the Pacific.

panthalassa.org/the-bruges-whale-project

You can adopt a Moray Firth dolphin, or a humpback whale, through WDC.

For more information on this and on WDC's whale and dolphin Shorewatch programme, please go to: **uk.whales.org**

Meet the real
whale watchers

Hi, I'm Vicki, I study whales, dolphins and porpoises and my work helps showcase how important these animals are in combatting climate change. On the next few pages, you'll find out exactly why whales are so amazing as this science is explained.

Seeing whales and dolphins in the wild is an unforgettable experience, just remember that if you go out on a whale-watching trip, choose an operator that follows a code of conduct to behave responsibly around the animals to ensure they aren't disturbed. And if you have a dog with you whilst you're out in nature, remember to keep it on a lead and under control at all times as they can frighten all types of wildlife.

Vicki James
Whale and Dolphin Researcher

Hello, I'm Carla and my job is to protect whales and dolphins. Animals can't save themselves, so we need to make sure that everything we do - from what we eat, buy and use - isn't harmful to them. Plastic that makes its way into the oceans is particularly dangerous because it carries toxic chemicals so it's important that we avoid unnecessary and single-use plastic, and reduce, reuse and recycle the plastic we do use.

The best part of my job is knowing that what I do can make a difference to encourage people to protect whales and dolphins. Find out what you can do to help on the next pages.

Dr Carla Boreham
Whale and Dolphin Campaign Leader

The science
behind the story

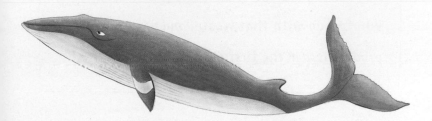

Human impact on the planet

Like, Finn, Jesse and Skye, lots of young people today feel strongly about the impact we have on our world and want to make a positive change.

Humans are producing more throwaway waste than ever. In the past 100 years, the waste we produce has increased 10 times and our planet is suffering. Everything we do creates waste. We are beginning to think more carefully about what to do with that waste, and how we can produce less in the first place.

Some natural materials like paper, cotton and wool can **biodegrade** and become part of the earth (including items such as clothes, magazines, books and bedding). Some synthetic materials are so strong that they don't biodegrade and this can be a problem. Plastic is a useful material. It is strong, waterproof and lasts a long time. It can be used for all sorts of amazing things which make our lives easier such as plastic bottles, carrier bags, bottles for cleaning products and much more, and can be reused again and again. But what happens to it when we don't need it any more? This is when plastic becomes a concern, because it doesn't biodegrade, but breaks into smaller and smaller pieces (microplastics) which stay on our planet for over 450 years. And we are throwing away more and more of it, including single-use plastics which we use only once before we throw away. So where does it all go?

Impact of single-use plastics on our planet

We usually throw away our rubbish into a bin, which gets emptied into a bigger bin and then collected regularly by bin lorries. Lots of items can be sorted for recycling and are taken to recycling plants to be made into something else. This is great when it's clear what can be recycled but sometimes it's tricky to know what to include in which recycling bin, or whether to leave a lid on or not. Some items can't be recycled and these are emptied into landfill sites which are big holes in the ground, outside our towns and cities. This waste causes many problems for the environment, including releasing gases which are harmful to the ozone layer and contribute to climate change.

Some waste isn't put into a bin or gets blown out of landfill sites. When plastic waste ends up in our natural environment, it causes harm. This is called pollution. If plastic is eaten by an animal, it is harmful. Animals and birds get tangled in plastic and can't move properly to feed or escape from predators which can lead to injury or even death. When animals, birds and plants die, this impacts our environment and this is why reducing single-use plastic waste has become such an important topic for us to consider in trying to help our planet.

9% of plastic is recycled

12% of plastic is burnt, which releases harmful gases

79% is buried in landfill or dumped on land or at sea

Human impact on the planet: climate change

What effect does all this plastic waste have on our environment? When plastic is produced, and transported, it produces a gas called carbon dioxide or CO_2. Sometimes plastic is burned to dispose of it, and this produces even more CO_2. Carbon dioxide is a greenhouse gas which is a gas that traps heat on our planet – it works like a greenhouse. Greenhouses keep plants warm, and greenhouse gases keep our planet warm. We need our planet to be warm enough so that all the living things on it can live. Without greenhouse gases, Earth would be too cold for anything to survive. We need some greenhouse gases. But when we do things

like burning plastic, we add more greenhouse gases around our planet, which trap too much heat and make our planet too warm. When we trap too many greenhouse gases, the temperature of our planet rises and causes changes to our weather (like drought or flooding, melting ice and stronger winds). This is called climate change and affects every living thing on Earth.

Human impact on the planet: climate change

There are many things that contribute to climate change. One of the most important ways we can help to slow down the rate of climate change is to decrease the things we do on our planet that give off carbon dioxide and increase the things that absorb carbon dioxide.

We saw above that reducing the amount of single-use plastic we use, reusing what we can and finally recycling anything left over, can help lower the amount of carbon dioxide we produce. Lots of living things on our planet also help by absorbing carbon dioxide, including trees and plants, as well as animals.

Many of us on our planet are working hard to reduce climate change. But did you know that whales in particular have a very important role to play? Despite their bluey grey appearance, we could say that because of their eco-work, whales are actually very green!

Where in the world are whales found?

Whales live in all the oceans of the world and can be found from the poles to the equator. The whales in the story are found in the Moray Firth in the North Sea, near to Inverness in Scotland, UK. Some whales move through the oceans at different times of year which is called migration. They might migrate to feed in one area, then to breed in another.

Every whale counts: how many whales are there?

Around 28 different species of whales and dolphins can be seen around the UK coastline. Arrow, the whale in the story, is a minke whale. Jesse's favourite whale is a humpback whale.

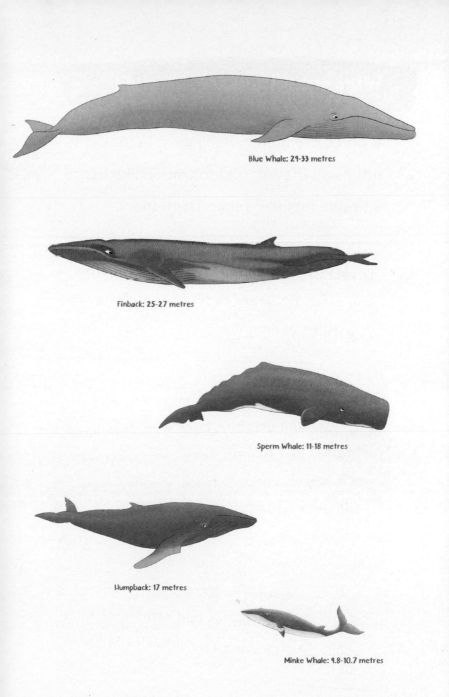

Blue Whale: 29-33 metres

Finback: 25-27 metres

Sperm Whale: 11-18 metres

Humpback: 17 metres

Minke Whale: 9.8-10.7 metres

Why are whales so special?

Whales are mammals like us. In fact, although they don't look much like us, we have lots in common with them:

It takes the majority of baby sperm whales and orcas 1-2 years to learn their language - just like our toddlers.

Whales and dolphins have well-developed brains, just like us. They can recognise, remember, communicate, problem-solve and understand.

Some live in families and communities where they have different roles to play.

They breathe air like us and give birth to live young (calves). Mothers also produce milk and whales have hair too!

Whales and dolphins enjoy one another's company and some play together, just like us.

They're communication experts – some are chatty and they can all communicate in interesting and novel ways.

Whale pump

How do whales actually help our environment? Mum mentions whale poo which is scientifically called the "whale pump". To find out what it is, we have to descend to the depths of the ocean.

Across all the species, whales eat prey at all depths of the ocean and excrete nutrient rich poo (faeces) when they return to the surface to breathe. The nutrients

in the poo help phytoplankton grow, which
are tiny, marine plants that absorb carbon
dioxide which dissolves into the ocean
from the air, and then release oxygen.
Whales help provide oxygen
for all the life in the ocean to breathe.
Some of this oxygen escapes into the air
and over millions of years, has provided
up to half the oxygen in the air. Remember
– we need oxygen to breathe! We owe
every other breath to the ocean.
The more whales there are,
the more phytoplankton there are,
the more carbon is taken out of
the atmosphere and the more
oxygen is released to ocean life.
That's great for our planet!

Ocean soup: the whale conveyor belt

Minke whales migrate – they make seasonal migration journeys between summer feeding grounds in cold seas and warmer breeding grounds during the winter. Their feeding grounds are in the cold polar seas where there are plenty of fish. But this colder environment would be more challenging for newborn whales. Minke whales make the best of both worlds by feeding in the cold-water areas in the summer months, then swimming to the warmer water to have their babies.

When they travel across the oceans, whales release lots of nutrients from their bodies, in addition to their poo, like wee and skin, which is perfect for other animals

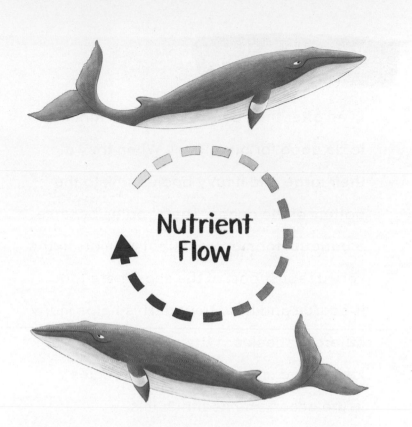

Nutrient
Flow

to feed on. Because whales also travel
frequently from the surface of the water
to the depths of the ocean, they help mix
all the nutrients which is essential for lots
of different species in the oceans to live,
a bit like an ocean soup!

Whale fall

Even after their death, whales continue to do good for our planet. When they die, their large and heavy bodies sink to the bottom of the ocean. Their bodies become a banquet for many different animals in the very deepest part of the sea, where food is scarce and hard to find. This helps many different species in the ocean live for longer and multiply. The more species in the ocean, the healthier it is.

Whales help our climate in another way when they die. They collect carbon in their body cells during their long lives. When whales die, this carbon is locked away for centuries. It is not released into the atmosphere and so doesn't contribute to climate change.

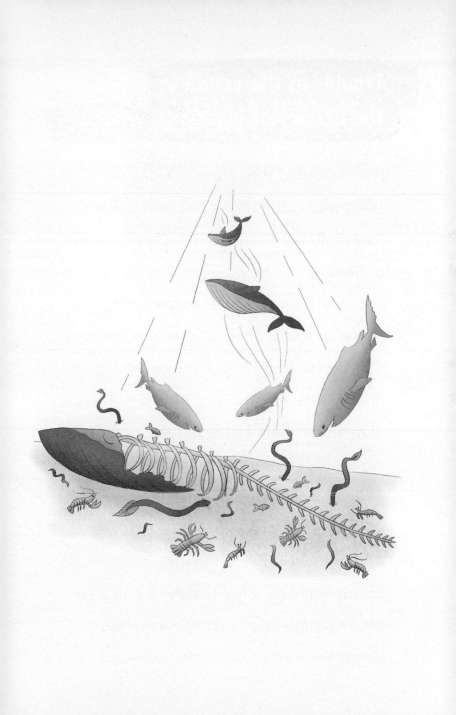

Trouble in the ocean: the impact of plastic on whales

It is estimated that plastics make up 60-80% of marine litter found in our oceans (International Union for the Conservation of Nature).

Like the minke whale, Arrow, which Finn, Jesse and Skye save, whales are in danger from plastic items that become entangled around their mouths, fins and tails. This can stop whales being able to feed, dive or move properly which can make it very difficult to find enough food to eat and reach the surface to breathe. Sadly, whales and other marine animals can also accidentally eat plastics which can also cause severe injuries and sometimes death. For some whale species, such as orcas and sperm whales who live in tight social units, when even one whale dies, its family and the whale community who rely on it also suffer.

Once plastic gets into the ocean, it eventually breaks down into tiny pieces called microplastics. They are small enough that many marine animals eat them accidentally. This can lead to injury or death in the animal.

Microplastics can interfere with the amount of carbon absorbed by the ocean. Microplastics floating on the ocean surface also stop light travelling into the ocean which phytoplankton need to be able to grow. The microplastics also slow down the flow of oxygen from the ocean into the atmosphere.

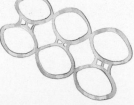

Every bottle makes a difference

Finn starts out by being really anxious about plastics in the oceans and how it impacts whales. It feels like an overwhelming job, and too big for little actions to make a difference. This is called climate anxiety.

What he realises by the end is that our little actions when joined together make a big difference. He feels less anxious because he is actually doing something to help. What can we do?

What you can do to help in the short term: changes at home

Reduce

- [ ] Use less disposable plastic in our day to day lives. Choose alternatives made of natural materials like wood, cardboard, paper and cotton.

- [ ] Use a BRITA water filter at home instead of buying plastic bottles of water.

- [ ] Try not to buy things you only use once – or think of another way to use them.

- [ ] Aim for plastic-free birthday parties. Choose paper party bags, cotton fabric bunting and paper streamers, and forget the balloons!

- [ ] Use containers, pots or brown paper bags for sandwiches and snacks.

☐ Avoid buying items wrapped in lots of plastic. Could you use fabric bags for fruit and veg instead?

☐ Use beeswax wraps instead of clingfilm to protect foods.

☐ Choose clothes made from natural fabrics.

Reuse

☐ Use a refillable water bottle – like the BRITA filter one.

☐ Choose a reusable lunchbox.

☐ Use reusable shopping bags.

☐ Reuse items of clothing by cutting and sewing.

Recycle

☐ Once plastic can't be reused any more, check the symbols on the label to see if it can be recycled and place it in the correct recycling bin. You can take your used BRITA filter to your closest recycling point.

☐ Pick up plastic litter we find in our towns and on the beach – and put in the recycling bin to stop it getting into rivers and into the sea.

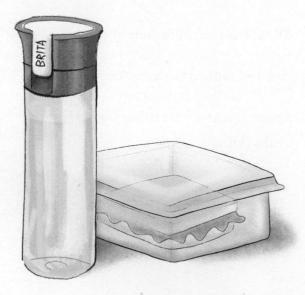

Where you can make a difference in other areas

☐ Educate those around us about environmental issues like Jesse does on the train. But remember, no one is perfect and every little helps.

☐ Choose to take the train, rather than fly like Finn and Jesse's family do.

☐ If you find an injured animal, ask for help from experts, keep quiet around the animal so as not to distress it further, and be proud that you have tried to help, even if it doesn't end the way you hoped.

☐ Fundraise for important wildlife charities.

☐ Volunteer at a local wildlife centre.

☐ Adopt a whale, dolphin or orca with Whale and Dolphin Conservation to help protect these amazing creatures.

Do you want to be a whale watcher?

If you are inspired, like Finn and Jesse's mum, to spend your working life helping animals and the natural environment, maybe one of these jobs would suit you in the future. If you are interested, the best thing you can do right now is to find out as much as you can about the area you're interested in by talking to people, reading, watching documentaries and maybe even volunteering near home.

Careers

Marine biologist:

Studies the ocean and the animals and plants that live in it. You might research living things in the ocean, teach other people and you would be learning all the time.

Conservationist:

Someone who protects the environment and wildlife. Your job would be to save animals or plants, protect an area of the world or teach people how to preserve nature and the environment.

Careers

Environmental scientist:

You would use your knowledge of science to protect the environment. You may clean up polluted areas, advise people who make laws, or work with businesses to reduce waste.

Fundraisers:

You might work for a charity, like Whale and Dolphin Conservation, to help raise money for projects that protect whales and dolphins around the world. You would enjoy talking to people and persuading them of your goals.

What's next for whales?

Much of the information about whales in this book has come from Whale and Dolphin Conservation (WDC) which is the leading charity for the protection of whales and dolphins.

WDC's aims:

- Stop hunting whales and dolphins.
- Prevent whales and dolphins dying in fishing nets.
- End cruel whale and dolphin captivity.
- Create safer seas.

There are many ways you can support WDC, including learning about whales and dolphins and fundraising. You could join the WDC team at uk.whales.org/kidzone and become a "Dolphin Defender".

WDC hopes that one day we will celebrate whale and dolphin rights being recognised in law. When these rights are recognised, whales will be protected. It is important that we look after these amazing animals for their own sake.

As Finn and Jesse's mum knows, the most important job to do is to watch whales and dolphins to learn more about them. WDC has many resources via whales.org to help you learn more about how to protect these amazing animals who do so much good for our planet.

Whales help us so much in our quest to reduce climate change across the world.

New words, explained

Glossary

Baleen A filter-feeding system inside the mouths of baleen whales. Baleen plates filter out small fish and krill from seawater.

Biodegrade The breakdown of a substance or object by bacteria or other living microorganisms.

Bottlenose dolphins A species of dolphin with a distinct bottle-shaped nose, found in tropical and temperate waters throughout the world.

Carbon dioxide A colourless and odourless gas made up of carbon and oxygen.

Carbon footprint The total amount of carbon dioxide and other greenhouse gases produced by a single person, organisation, product or process.

Carcass The body of a dead animal.

Climate anxiety Fear or distress caused by the consequences of climate change and the future of the planet.

Climate change A change in global and regional climate patterns attributed to an increase in atmospheric carbon dioxide from the burning of fossil fuels.

Dorsal fin Fin located on the back of whales, dolphins and fish.

Fossil fuels A natural fuel such as coal or gas, formed in the geological past from the remains of living organisms.

Greenhouse gas Any atmospheric gas that absorbs and emits radiant energy and contributes to the greenhouse effect.

Juvenile whale A young whale, larger than a calf (baby whale) but not yet an adult.

Kestrels A small falcon that hovers in the air with its head to the wind.

Kittiwakes A small gull that nests in colonies on sea cliffs, having a loud call that resembles its name.

Landfill A method of building up land and disposing of solid waste by burying it underground.

Marine biologist Someone who studies the biology of marine life, organisms and plants in oceans so they can protect them.

Microplastic Tiny pieces or particles of plastic in the environment resulting from the disposal and breakdown of consumer products and industrial plastic waste.

Migration The regular, usually seasonal, movement of all or part of an animal population to and from a given area.

Minke whales A small, fast swimming baleen whale with a distinct dark grey back and white belly. They are found all over the world and prefer cooler seas and can be seen off the coast of Scotland, the Northern Atlantic and Pacific Oceans.

Nutrients A substance in food that provides essential nourishment for people, animals and plants to live and grow.

Ospreys A large fish-eating bird of prey with long, narrow wings and a white underside and crown.

Oxygen A colourless, odourless reactive gas which is the life-supporting component of the air we breathe.